JUV/E
FIC
W9-BBU-870
In the piney woods

# In the Piney Woods

☆ RONI SCHOTTER ☆

PICTURES BY KIMBERLY BULCKEN ROOT

MELANIE KROUPA BOOKS

FARRAR, STRAUS AND GIROUX ☆ NEW YORK

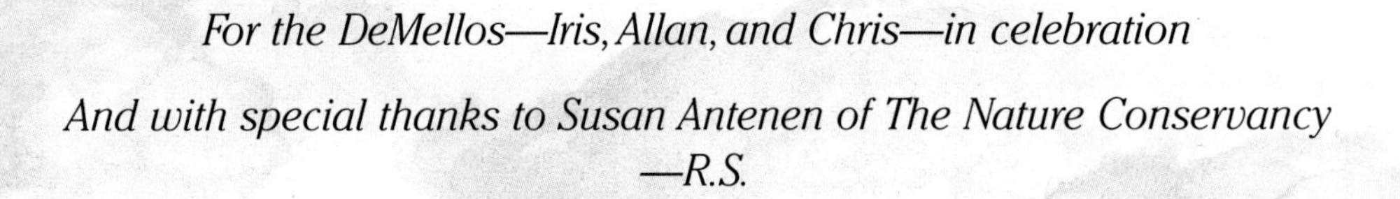

*For the DeMellos—Iris, Allan, and Chris—in celebration*

*And with special thanks to Susan Antenen of The Nature Conservancy*
*—R.S.*

*In loving memory of Ernest Knott Linker*
*—K.B.R.*


Distributed in Canada by Douglas & McIntyre Ltd.
Color separations by Chroma Graphics PTE Ltd.
Printed and bound in China by South China Printing Company Limited
Designed by Jennifer Browne
First edition, 2003
1 3 5 7 9 10 8 6 4 2

Library of Congress Cataloging-in-Publication Data
Schotter, Roni.
In the piney woods / by Roni Schotter ; pictures by Kimberly Bulcken Root.
p. cm.
Summary: Grandpa and his granddaughter spend his last summer visiting and enjoying the pine woods near their house.
ISBN 0-374-33623-7
[1. Pine—Fiction. 2. Trees—Fiction. 3. Grandfathers—Fiction. 4. Death—Fiction.] I. Root, Kimberly Bulcken, ill. II. Title.

PZ7.S3765 In 2002
[E]—dc21
2001029383

Long before I was born, Grandpa, strong and straight and singing, built our little house at the edge of the sandy, piney woods, near the sea.

Many years later, crowded and close, we all live together there—Grandpa and I, Mama and Papa, and Big Sister Sada with Sam and their baby that is growing, round and ripe inside her.

But Grandpa is old now. No longer does he sing. His body is bent like the branches of the low pines and scrub oaks that grow in the pine barrens near our house where Grandpa and I love to walk. His words are few, each one special.

"Sun breath," Grandpa says to me, smiling and sniffing the morning air. "Go, Ella girl? Now?"

"Yes," I agree. The sun feels warm as a wool coat. Perfect for a walk in the woods. "Give me your arm," I say. When I was small, Grandpa helped me walk. Now I help *him* walk.

Philly

Among the crooked dwarf pitch pines and the gnarled scrub oaks, Grandpa and I play our game. We turn and twist and pretend we two are trees. We stand very still and feel the hot sun and the cool sea breeze blow across our bark.

Cafe

When we're done, we poke the sandy soil, Grandpa with his cane, and I with my feet. "No room," Grandpa says, looking worried.

"Yes," I say, knowing just what he means. The trees are old and the forest floor thick with dead branches and needles. No room for new baby trees to push down young root legs and grow.

We peer at pinecones. "Fire bursts" we call them. When I was small, Grandpa first taught me about the tightly closed cones of the dwarf pitch pines. Cupping our hands together, we look at one.

"Waiting," Grandpa whispers, and again I know what he means. Locked inside each special cone, seeds are patiently waiting to burst free, but only fire is hot enough to melt the sticky, pitch-piney glue that holds them tight together. Without fire, the seeds can't get out. And without fire to clear a space on the crowded forest floor, there's no room for the seeds to sprout.

"Waiting," Grandpa repeats as he has so many times before. "Everything has its time."

High above us a harrier hawk sails on a sea breeze. I forget about fire, pinecones—everything—while Grandpa and I gather hats full of berries blue as summer evenings, sweet as summer days.

That night Grandpa and I stay up late with Mama and Papa, Sada and Sam, turning blueberries into pie and muffins and jam. Sada eats everything—the baby growing inside her must be a hungry one!

The next morning Grandpa is too tired to go to the pinewoods. His old legs are wobbly and weak. He lends me his cane for a walking stick, and Sada and I go together. Sada rests below while I climb into the trembling branches of an old oak. Its dry leaves rattle in the sea breeze, and its ancient arms hold me up and close and nearer the sky. I pretend I am a nestle bird and call down to Sada below, “Caroo-caroo!”

“Caroo-caroo,” Sada answers back, and I wonder if, far away, Grandpa can hear us.

CAPT JOHN
CHATTERS

One gusty, gray day, Grandpa and I sit on the porch rocking with the wind and listening to the grumble of dark clouds in the distance. We pretend we two are storms. We make fierce faces, shake our fists, and grumble back at the sky.

When the angry clouds roll in, Grandpa and I go inside where Mama's teakettle boils and rattles like the world outside.

Safe and together, we crowd at the window to watch—Grandpa and I, Mama and Papa, Big Sister Sada with her even bigger belly, and Sam.

The clouds hurl crooked spears of lightning at the earth, but Grandpa's eyes are on something far away. The sky flashes and crackles and booms so loud the whole house shakes . . . and then it happens . . . a sizzle, a hiss, and a burst of flame.

"Fire in the pinewoods!" Papa yells, reaching for a shovel and a raincoat and running out the door. Sam is right beside him.

"Wait for me!" I call out.

Papa stops and looks at Mama with a question in his eyes. She looks at Grandpa, who smiles at me and nods. "Go, Ella!" he says. "Go for me!" I hear his thrilling words over thunder and the screech of sirens.

In the pinewoods, jagged flames leap up and lick the trees like great fiery dragons. Rabbits run to safety. Snakes slither away. Firefighters are at work with hoses and shovels. Papa, Sam, and I dig with them, for many long hours, a ditch that fire cannot cross. My arms ache, but I keep on digging. The world is hot and piney, smoky and wet. It is raining. The storm clouds that started the fire are helping to end it now with hard, cheek-slapping rain.

I feel so tired I think I am dreaming. Am I? Suddenly, by my foot, I see a pitch pinecone, singed by the fire, its sticky glue melted. Wide open, its seeds are, at last, unlocked! I pick it up carefully, for it is still warm. I hold it gently against my chest. There is someone I want to show it to, someone who's been waiting to see it a long, long time . . .

Grandpa sleeps in his chair by the window. He looks so terribly tired. Well, I think, long life has tired him out. “Grandpa,” I call, unable to keep still, “I’ve brought you something!”

Grandpa’s dark eyes open and stare out at me like the seeds of the special treasure I have for him. “At last,” he says, quietly. “Good girl!” We kiss good night, and Grandpa falls asleep smiling, holding our treasure in his hands.

AMERICA
SHAD
SHRIM
PALAC
CAPT'S
TABLE

In the morning I want to take Grandpa to the piney woods, but his legs aren't working well, so Papa and Sam make themselves into a chair, and Sada and Mama, armrests. I am the guide. Together we make a grand procession!

That is the last day Grandpa and I spend in the pinewoods. For the rest of summer Grandpa is too tired, even to be carried. He sits in his chair by the window, and I tell him the stories he has told me about the pinewoods and the days before I was born when he was young and strong and singing. Sometimes he sleeps, and his breath whistles like the wind in the pines, and sometimes he wakes, but always he is smiling.

On a day in autumn when the damp earth smells like salt and pepper and the falling leaves do their last, wild dance, Grandpa dies, and I've lost my best friend. Everything has its time, I know he would tell me, but his words don't help. We bury Grandpa at the edge of our land near the pinewoods. I take a seed from the open pitch pinecone I brought him, and plant it by his grave.

Then I run faster than a deer into the pinewoods. "Let her go," I hear Papa say to Mama on the wind. I have not been to the pinewoods since the last time with Grandpa. The burnt pines are sad ghost trees now, skinny skeletons. There is room at last on the forest floor for new baby trees to poke down their young root legs and grow, but I don't care, because Grandpa isn't there to see it.

There are a few trees that the fire hasn't touched. I climb the tallest of them. "Caroo-caroo!" I call as loud as I can. "Caroo-*caroo*!" I wonder if, far away, Grandpa can hear me.

Many sad months have passed, and it is spring now. Under the scorched branches of the dwarf pitch pines, a miracle! Tiny trees are rising, green and strong and straight. Out of the roots of the scrub oaks, long stems of glowing green leaves have sprouted. Close by Grandpa's grave, a baby pitch pine is bravely pushing its way into the world.

In the room that once was Grandpa's, our baby, my new nephew, is growing strong and straight and singing. In a few years I will take him to the pinewoods, and we will play the game that Grandpa and I used to play. I will teach him everything Grandpa taught me about the tightly closed cones of the dwarf pitch pines—how patiently they are waiting for *their* chance to burst free and be.

FRESH
BOX

SHRIMP